SABAN'S MIGHTY MORPHIN POWER RANGERS ™

LORD ZEDD STRIKES BACK!

By Jean Waricha

D1411786

A PARACHUTE PRESS BOOK

GROSSET & DUNLAP • NEW YORK

A PARACHUTE PRESS BOOK
Parachute Press, Inc.
156 Fifth Avenue
New York, NY 10010

Published by Grosset & Dunlap, Inc., a member of The Putnam &
Grosset Group, New York. GROSSET & DUNLAP is a trademark of
Grosset & Dunlap, Inc. Published simultaneously in Canada.

Creative Consultant: Cheryl Saban.

With special thanks to Cheryl Saban, Ban Pryor, and Sherry Stack.

Printed in the U.S.A.
April 1995
Library of Congress Catalog Card Number : 94-74529
ISBN: 0-448-40952-6
A B C D E F G H I J

Go, go, Power Rangers!

Jason, Kimberly, Tommy, Zack, and Billy were five ordinary teenagers—until they met Zordon, a good wizard trapped in another dimension. Zordon gave each teenager incredible power to morph into action and super-strength to battle the forces of Evil on Earth.

Tommy, the sixth teenager to join the Power Rangers, received his superpowers from the evil Rita Repulsa. Then she tricked him into carrying out her wicked deeds. But once Tommy met the Power Rangers, he joined them in the fight against Evil!

Together these six powerful protectors will stop at nothing to save the Earth! So beware evil forces—the Power Rangers are here to stay!

CHAPTER 1

The hills just outside of Angel Grove were usually quiet. Very quiet. But not today.

Today the shouts and cheering of kids getting ready to race filled the air.

"Welcome to the Children's Hospital Motor Marathon!" an announcer's voice boomed.

Kids from all over town had come to compete. Among the riders were six special teenagers—Jason, Kimberly, Tommy, Trini, Billy, and Zack. These six teenagers didn't look any different from the others—but they were.

When trouble threatened, they changed into the Mighty Morphin Power Rangers. Together they used their special superpowers to fight the forces of Evil.

But today the six friends *weren't* going to use their superpowers. They were in a race to help raise money for the Children's Hospital. They wanted to compete fair and square.

Trini zipped up her yellow jacket

and flipped her black ponytail over her shoulder. "This is great!" she exclaimed. "Having a good time—for a good cause."

"You said it," Zack agreed, tying on a purple bandanna. "I can't wait to hit those trails."

"Get ready to hit the *dirt!*" someone snarled behind them.

Zack and Trini turned to see Bulk, Angel Grove's biggest troublemaker, and his skinny sidekick, Skull. They were dressed in black from head to toe. Black leather jackets. Black pants. Black boots. Only Bulk's black helmet showed the slightest bit of color. Red, blue, yellow, and purple sparkled all over it!

"Yeah," Skull piped up. "You'll be eating our dust all the way across the finish line."

"Oh, *puh-lease*," Kimberly said, pulling back her shoulder-length brown hair with a pink ribbon. "This race is not about winning. It's about helping children."

"Yeah, sure," Bulk sneered. "Remember *that* when you lose."

Bulk and Skull snickered as they slithered off to find their four-wheelers.

Tommy and Jason turned to their four-wheelers to make final safety checks. Then Billy rolled up the maps showing the race route.

"Okay, guys. It's time!" Tommy

exclaimed. "Let's head over to the starting line!"

Rita Repulsa jumped up and down on the balcony of her palace on the moon. As always the Empress of Evil was spying on the six teenagers through her repulsascope.

"Those Power Rangers are right where we want them!" she cried with wicked delight. "Goldar! Squatt! Baboo! Come here!"

As her bumbling servants scurried over, a black cloud drifted above the palace.

Then a crack of thunder split the air, and lightning bolts zigzagged across the sky. Rita's entire fortress shuddered.

Goldar, Squatt, and Baboo clutched each other in terror. Even Rita clung to her repulsa-scope in fear. The dark cloud parted, and a horrible image began to form.

Oh, no! Rita knew that shape. It was Lord Zedd—the Emperor of all the forces of Evil! His huge body looked like raw red muscle bound by silver armor. Thin, clear tubes of gurgling liquid snaked around his arms and legs. No one had ever seen his face, because he hid it behind a silver mask.

It was Lord Zedd who had ordered Rita to destroy Earth. But Earth had the Power Rangers, six powerful protectors, and Rita had failed.

"You have not carried out your mission," Lord Zedd bellowed in a deep, raspy voice. "I have come to change all that—immediately!"

Lord Zedd's image formed into a glowing ball of fire. Like a comet, it streaked through the palace, then disappeared.

"He's going to ruin everything," Rita whined.

"But wh-where is he?" stammered Baboo, glancing around.

"Where he belongs," said Goldar. "In this palace! In his old Chamber of Command!"

"Ohhh! I've got such a headache!" Rita moaned.

"I'm going to greet my real emperor!" Goldar announced, shoving past Rita.

"Maybe we should check this guy out," Baboo agreed.

"Hey!" Rita cried. "Wait for me!"

Meanwhile, back in Angel Grove, the announcer shouted, "On your marks, get set, go!"

The motor marathon was on! Teenagers in cool helmets and riding gear roared over the starting line, down the dirt trails.

BOOM! Thunder announcing Lord Zedd's arrival on the moon echoed all the way down to Earth. It shook the ground and drowned out the moaning sound of the four-wheelers' motors.

"What was that?" Jason glanced at the sky, then signaled his friends to stop. They pulled off the trail and skidded to a halt.

"Did you hear that?" Zack asked.

Billy scanned the rumbling sky. "It might be thunder...but somehow I don't think so."

Suddenly the communicator on Jason's wrist beeped.

"Power Rangers!" came a low voice. "You must transport to the Command Center at once!"

"What's going on?" Trini asked.

"I don't know," said Jason, frowning in concern. "But it sounds like trouble. Big trouble."

CHAPTER 2

Six ordinary teens turned into six columns of sparkling colored light that streaked across the sky over the desert. They traveled to their secret headquarters—the Command Center—and materialized as Jason, Kimberly, Zack, Trini, Tommy, and Billy.

The Command Center echoed

with the sounds of buzzing computers and the frantic cries of a small robot named Alpha 5.

"What's wrong?" Jason asked Alpha 5 and Zordon. Zordon was the good wizard who gave the Power Rangers their superpowers. He guided them in their fight against Evil.

Zordon's pale face wavered in a column of eerie green light as he began to explain. "The thing I have feared the most has happened. Lord Zedd has returned."

"Who's Lord Zedd?" Billy asked.

"Rita's lord and master," Zordon answered grimly.

"You mean there's somebody *worse* than Rita?" Kimberly asked, shuddering at the thought.

"I'm afraid so. Lord Zedd has been living in darker places in another galaxy. Eons ago he put Rita in charge of carrying out his plan to destroy the Earth. Since she has failed..."

"He's come back to finish the job!" Trini said.

"But we can defeat him, right?" Tommy asked.

"I do not know, Rangers," Zordon said.

The Power Rangers stared at the wizard in surprise.

Zordon shook his head sadly. "I'm afraid not even the power of the Zords may be enough to defeat Lord Zedd's evil magic."

* * *

Back on the moon, bolt after bolt of lightning lit up the palace like a pinball machine. In the very center of it all sat Lord Zedd on a carved stone throne. He was definitely back in control.

Goldar entered to see his new emperor petting a huge boa constrictor curled around his body. Lord Zedd lifted the snake and held it high. Magically it changed into a silver staff. A large sparkling *Z* flashed at the top.

Goldar bowed before Zedd's monstrous metal boots. "Welcome back, My Emperor! I am here to serve and obey only you!"

"Your spineless, sniveling attitude leads me to believe that you will serve me well," Lord Zedd said. "For that I will give back to you what was once taken away."

Lightning flashed from Zedd's staff. In an instant, huge black wings appeared on Goldar's back.

"Thank you, master!" Goldar cried. "I won't forget this."

Just then Rita barged in. "Oh, Lord Zedd! How nice of you to come. What a pleasant surprise."

"Silence!" Lord Zedd bellowed. "You have made me very angry." As he spoke these words, something very mysterious happened. The room glowed a bright red!

Rita trembled. "Oh, please," she begged. "Please give me another chance to destroy Earth!"

Squatt and Baboo were huddled behind a wall. They spied on Rita and Zedd through a peephole. "Amazing!" Squatt said. "The Chamber of Command seems to change color to match Lord Zedd's mood!"

The Emperor of Evil pointed his staff at Rita. A mighty bolt of lightning struck her, and she began to shrink. Smaller and smaller. Until she was the size of a little doll.

With a beastly laugh, Goldar popped her into what looked like a trash can carved from stone. He slammed the lid shut.

"Let me out of here! I can't stand small spaces!" Rita cried in a tiny voice. But no one listened.

Zedd ordered his soldiers—mindless creatures called Super Putties—to fling Rita far into space. His cold laughter turned the room an icy blue.

When Rita had disappeared from sight, Zedd roared for his Super Putties. Zedd's warriors were far stronger than Rita's Putties. Each one had a large *Z* carved on its chest.

"The Power Rangers will never guess my Super Putties' secret!" Zedd boomed. Then he commanded his warriors, "Go to the mountains of Earth and finish off those puny Rangers—once and for all!"

CHAPTER 3

Back on Earth, Bulk and Skull roared down the trail on their four-wheelers until…

BOOM! A deafening thunder-bolt cracked right above them.

Skull's head jerked up—so he didn't see the big rock in the road ahead.

CRUNCH! His bike hit the rock,

and he flew over the handlebars. A second later Bulk's four-wheeler slammed into Skull's. *CRACK!* Bulk soared through the air. They both landed in a prickly tree.

"Now look what you've done!" Bulk growled at Skull.

The two tumbled down from the tree and stumbled over to check their four-wheelers. Both were wrecked.

"Oh, great," said Bulk. "Now what do we do?"

Another thunderbolt blasted across the sky.

"Let's get out of here!" they cried, hurrying off on foot.

Soon they came upon six deserted four-wheelers.

"Hey, it's Jason and his geek friends' four-wheelers! What luck!" crowed Skull.

"Let's cruise!" Bulk snickered.

As they hopped on the four-wheelers, Lord Zedd's Super Putties appeared out of nowhere.

The Putties surrounded them. Bulk shrieked. Skull jumped into Bulk's arms. "Save me, Bulky!"

The Super Putties moved in closer and closer....

Back at the Command Center, the sound of an alarm split the air. "Aye-yi-yi-yi-yi!" Alpha cried. "Power Rangers! Look!"

He pointed to the viewing globe, a large crystal ball that

showed scenes on Earth. The six teenagers crowded around it.

"It's Bulk and Skull," said Billy. "Putties are attacking them!"

Kimberly squinted. "They don't look like *regular* Putties."

"They are Zedd's new Super Putties," Zordon reported. "They will be much harder to defeat."

"Bulk and Skull are sitting on our four-wheelers," Zack cried. "I'll bet this attack was meant for us!"

"We've got to help them!" Trini said.

"Let's morph into action!" Jason shouted.

The Power Rangers quickly called out their dinosaurs' names. "Mastodon!" "Tyrannosaurus!"

"Triceratops!" "Saber-toothed Tiger!" "Pterodactyl!"

"Dragon!" cried Tommy, calling on his special spirit.

In an instant the six teens morphed into—the Power Rangers! Now they stood dressed in shining helmets and sleek jumpsuits—Tommy, the Green Ranger. Zack, the Black Ranger. Kimberly, the Pink Ranger. Billy, the Blue Ranger. Trini, the Yellow Ranger. And Jason, the Red Ranger.

Then they vanished—and reappeared on the mountain trail.

"The Power Rangers!" Bulk gasped.

"We're saved, Bulky boy!" Skull squeaked as the two ran off and ducked into the bushes.

The Power Rangers somersaulted into battle. Tommy landed a
hard kick to one Putty's leg, but
the warrior just brushed off the
blow. The other Power Rangers
karate chopped and kicked, but
they couldn't stop the Putties.
Zack took a punch and fell hard.

"They're too strong!" Trini
cried, tumbling into Jason.

"We can't give up," Jason said.
"We've got to figure out a weak-
ness."

Suddenly Tommy fell to his
knees in the dirt. He clutched his
chest. "My powers!" he gasped.
"They're weakening."

Two Putties grabbed him

roughly and flung him into the air. Tommy crashed into the brambles with a groan.

Jason tried to sprint to Tommy's side, but a Putty blocked his way. He took a deep breath, then directed all his strength into one big punch to the *Z* on the Putty's chest.

And something happened. The Putty glowed mysteriously, broke into chunks—and disappeared!

Jason shook his head in amazement, then shouted to the others. "Guys! I found their weak spot. Aim for the *Z!*"

The Power Rangers tried it, and within minutes each managed to hit a *Z*. It really worked! One by one the Putties glowed, crumbled, then vanished. Jason had discovered the Super Putties' secret!

"Hey, where are Bulk and Skull?" Billy asked, glancing around.

The two bumbleheads were still trembling in the bushes.

"You two!" Jason called, spotting them. "Are you all right?"

Speechless, Bulk and Skull just nodded, then managed to give the thumbs-up sign.

Jason turned back to the others. "Okay, guys, let's get back to the Command Center."

The six Power Rangers changed into crackling columns of colored light, then disappeared.

Bulk and Skull stared after the shimmering lights in disbelief. Their mouths hung open.

"Those..." gasped Bulk, "were the Power Rangers!"

"No one's gonna believe we saw them," Skull moaned.

Bulk tried to think fast. "We'll prove it."

"We will?" Skull asked.

"They're real people, man," said Bulk. "We heard their voices. We just gotta find out who those voices belong to!"

"Right!" Skull said. "Uh...how?"

Bulk slung an arm around his pal. "I've got a plan," he said with a sly grin. "This one is *really* gonna make us famous!"

CHAPTER 4

"**Those punk Rangers** think they're so smart," Lord Zedd roared as he glared down at the Earth. "But they won't be so smart when my new monster is through with them. My new monster will get rid of those teenagers forever!" He clenched his silver-tipped fingers. "Then the world will be mine. All mine!"

Lord Zedd raised his wicked staff. Bright red light flashed from its tip and spiraled down to Earth. The light struck a river, shot below the water's surface, and zapped a fish. One special fish—a dangerous, man-eating piranha.

Lord Zedd worked his evil magic on the piranha.

Moments later a horrible creature rose from the water with a cranky roar. It was half fish, half man—and totally frightening. It stood on two enormous green, scaly legs. One hundred razor-sharp teeth filled its huge, gaping mouth. It licked its lips as it scanned the rocky shores for the enemy—the Power Rangers.

BEEEEEP! An alarm shrieked in the Command Center.

"Power Rangers," Zordon instructed, "Lord Zedd has unleashed a terrifying monster on Earth. Its name is Pirhantis Head, and its mission is to destroy Angel Grove. You must stop it. However Tommy will have to stay here. Alpha and I will try to re-energize his powers."

Tommy lowered his eyes. He tried to hide his disappointment. "Good luck, guys," he called as the Power Rangers morphed to an alley in Angel Grove.

"Pee-uuu!" Kimberly shouted. A

The Power Rangers are competing in the Angel Grove Motor Marathon. Billy and Kimberly check out the race map.

Bulk and Skull are in the race, too!

Suddenly Zack, Jason, and Tommy hear a strange BOOM thunder across the sky. *There's trouble ahead*, Jason thinks.

Oh, no! Lord Zedd, Emperor of all Evil, is back!

Goldar has come to welcome Lord Zedd, who has just taken over Rita Repulsa's fortress on the moon.

Lord Zedd has ordered the Super Putties to stuff Rita into a Dumpster and fling her into orbit.

"I'm afraid not even the power of the Zords may be enough to defeat Lord Zedd's evil magic," Zordon reports.

The viewing globe at the Command Center shows Lord Zedd's new Super Putties attacking Bulk and Skull.

Power Rangers to the rescue! Jason discovers the only way to defeat a Super Putty—hit the *Z* carved on its chest!

Meanwhile, Lord Zedd sends his evil monster, Pirhantis Head, to Earth.

The Power Rangers give a big thumbs up—not even Pirhantis Head or Lord Zedd can stop them!

What a perfect day for the Power Rangers—they finished the motor marathon and saved the Earth again!

foul odor hung in the air. They followed it and soon spotted the Pirhantis Head monster. It stood atop a four-story building.

"Ever heard of a bath?" Kimberly shouted up at the ugly creature.

"Ah! The Power Rangers!" the scaly monster cried. "Watch this!" It raised a strange flute, shaped like a fish, to its fang-filled mouth. Then it turned toward a deserted skyscraper and blew.

Huge concrete slabs came crashing down, almost crushing the Power Rangers.

"The flute!" Billy cried. "It has awesome power!"

"We need Dinozord power—

and now!" Jason shouted.

The Rangers called out the names of their dinosaurs. The ground trembled as the dinosaur robots awoke.

Tyrannosaurus erupted from a steaming crack in the ground.

Mastodon broke through its cage of ice.

Triceratops charged across a scorching desert.

Saber-toothed Tiger leaped through a twisted jungle.

Pterodactyl erupted from the fires of a volcano.

Side by side the Dinozords raced like the wind to answer the call.

But Pirhantis Head merely

laughed. "I'm afraid this time you'll be left out in the cold," the monster roared. Then the cold-blooded creature blew the flute again.

A frosty white blast hit Saber-toothed Tiger, and the Zord froze solid in its tracks. Another blast froze Triceratops. Another stopped Mastodon and Pterodactyl. Four Zords down!

"Oh, man! The monster froze our Zords!" Zack cried, as Pirhantis Head advanced on them. "We're history!"

"Look!" Jason cried. "We're not defeated yet! Here comes Tyrannosaurus!"

"Dinozord power!" all five Power Rangers shouted together.

Tyrannosaurus stomped forward, obeying their command.

"Not so fast!" Pirhantis Head shouted. The monster blew three times on its fish flute. Blasts of fog struck the Dinozord, surrounding it with a cloudlike glow.

The Dinozord's eyes glowed weirdly. And suddenly it roared at the Power Rangers and blasted them with Dinozord fire.

"What's going on?" yelled Jason. "It's turned on us!"

"We need Tommy and his Dragonzord," cried Zack. "They're our only hope!"

Back at the Command Center, Alpha and Tommy watched the whole terrible scene on the viewing globe. "I've got to help them!" Tommy exclaimed.

"I can strengthen your powers for a time, Green Ranger," Zordon said. "But I do not know how long the power will last."

"I'll take that risk," Tommy said. "The others need me."

Zordon zapped Tommy with extra power.

"I'm outta here," the Green Ranger yelled.

Seconds later Tommy appeared just as the other Power Rangers ducked another stream of Dinozord fire.

"That fish-face froze our Zords!" Zack shouted to Tommy.

"And watch out for Tyrannosaurus!" Trini warned.

"Don't worry," said Tommy. "I'll call up Dragonzord to protect us." He pulled his sword from his belt and held it up to his mouth. He played the secret melody that awoke the Dragonzord. With a mighty roar, Dragonzord rose from the depths of the sea.

The two gigantic Zords clashed together. *Clang! Clung! Zang!* Dragonzord lashed out with his enormous tail. The Dinozord flew backward and nearly fell over the four frozen Zords. Dragonzord and the Dinozord lunged forward. They fought fiercely while the Power Rangers watched helplessly. It was painful to see—a Zord fighting a Zord.

"It's not nice to fight your friends!" Pirhantis Head shouted. The monster played a tune on its flute and blasted Dragonzord. The Zord froze. Now an eerie glow shone from its eyes.

Tyrannosaurus and Dragonzord *both* turned to the Power Rangers, ready to attack!

"Oh, no. Not Dragonzord, too!" Trini yelled.

Bullets shot out from Dragonzord's tail, aimed straight at the Power Rangers. Built-in missiles fired from its fingertips.

Wang! Wang! Wang!

The Power Rangers somersaulted out of firing range, barely escaping the blasts.

Pirhantis Head belched a horrible laugh.

"We've got to get out of here!"

Jason cried. "Come on, guys!"

In a flash of sparkling light, the Power Rangers transported to the Command Center.

"Zordon, we've lost our Zords," Jason cried.

"I can't believe this is how it ends," Trini said sadly.

"Isn't there anything we can do?" Kimberly asked.

"I'm afraid nothing we could do would ever give the Zords enough power," Zordon answered. "Zedd is using thunder power. To fight back, you need new and more powerful Zords—equipped with the power of thunder!"

Alpha stepped forward, the lights on his shiny metal body

flashing. "Follow me, Power Rangers," the robot ordered. Then he led the Power Rangers outside to a windy, rocky hillside and pointed up to the stormy sky.

The Power Rangers stared into the dark clouds.

At first they heard only the sound of thunder in the distance. But one by one powerful creatures soared into view!

"Do not be alarmed, Power Rangers," Zordon's voice boomed. "These are your new Zords."

"Jason, you will control the Red Dragon Thunderzord. Its power is fierce and true. Trini, yours shall be the Griffin Thunderzord, swift and accurate. Zack, the Lion

Thunderzord, courageous and strong, will be yours. Billy, your Unicorn Thunderzord will have mythological powers and wisdom. Kimberly, take the Firebird Thunderzord, powerful and agile. When you join together these Thunderzords, they will form the Mega Thunderzord."

The Power Rangers stared in wonder at these new creations.

"Lord Zedd is in for it now!" Zack grinned widely.

But Kimberly's smile faded as she glanced at the Green Ranger. "What about Tommy?" she asked .

"We don't know yet if Tommy's powers will remain," Alpha explained. "We'll have to wait and see before we create a new Zord for him."

Tommy's powers had been weakened in an earlier fight with Rita. Now they were in danger of fading out forever.

"It's all right, guys," Tommy said, trying to smile. "We knew this might happen." He shrugged. "I just wish there were something I could do about it."

"When do we take control of the new Zords?" Trini asked.

"You must regain control of the old Zords first," Alpha said. "We need some of their parts to complete the new ones."

Jason shook his head. "But how will we ever do that?"

The Power Rangers dashed back to the Command Center. Alpha and Billy worked at the computer searching for a solution.

As Billy studied the screen, his face suddenly lit up. "I've got it! I can make a device that will jam Pirhantis Head's evil signal and

free our old Zords. But everything
I need is back at my lab."

"I'll go there with you," said
Trini. "Maybe I can help."

Trini and Billy vanished in a
sparkle of yellow and blue lights
just as the Command Center's
alarm rang again.

"Oh, no!" Alpha cried, pointing
to the viewing globe. "Pirhantis
Head is stomping toward the
Angel Grove Marathon."

"This is bad news," Zordon
announced. "Trini and Billy need
more time to create their signal
blocker."

"We can't wait," Jason said.
"We've got to morph!"

"But without your Zords,"

Zordon explained, "you can't defeat this monster. You might be hurt. The world cannot afford to lose you."

"But we can't let the monster hurt innocent kids!" Jason said.

"Let's go!" Zack cried.

Jason, Tommy, Zack, and Kim transported back to the mountain trail they had seen in the viewing globe. But where was Lord Zedd's monster?

"Hi, guys. Looking for something?" Pirhantis Head taunted from the top of a ridge.

"There it is!" shouted Jason. "That fish-face!"

"Now you see me," the monster shouted, "and now you don't!"

Poof! Pirhantis Head disappeared! And the Power Rangers were surrounded—by Lord Zedd's Super Putties!

Back at the race, Bulk and Skull were totally lost. Each blamed the other, and they grew so angry that they split up, riding in opposite directions. "Good thing I know where I'm going," Bulk muttered as he zoomed off.

"Huh!" Skull mumbled. "Bulk's going the wrong way."

Actually *both* of them were going the wrong way—around in a large circle! Soon they zoomed right toward each other, almost crashing when they met.

"What are you doing here?" they both yelled at once.

Then Skull's mouth dropped open as he stared over Bulk's shoulder. "Uh, Bulk? Are we near a river?"

"No," Bulk answered. "What's the matter with you?"

"B-behind you," Skull stuttered in a squeaky voice. "A f-fish! A huge, gigantic f-f-f-fish!"

Bulk slowly turned to meet the gaze of Pirhantis Head! "Going my way?" the monster cackled. Then it blew on its fish flute and blasted Bulk and Skull. Their four-wheelers took off fast—backward!

"Hel-l-lp!" they screamed as the bikes raced totally out of control.

* * *

Meanwhile the Power Rangers battled hard and sent the Super Putties back to Lord Zedd—in hundreds of tiny pieces! But there was no time to rest. Pirhantis Head had returned.

"Yoo-hoo!" the slimy creature called. The Power Rangers gaped in horror as the evil monster tooted its flute.

Dragonzord and Tyrannosaurus appeared at once. The Zords drew their mighty weapons. They blasted the ground with fireballs, stomping closer and closer to the kids on the trails.

Just then Billy and Trini appeared nearby with a large silver box—the signal blocker!

"Quick! Stop the Zords!" Jason called.

Billy aimed the signal blocker at Tyrannosaurus and Dragon-zord. Trini pushed the button to break Zedd's evil control.

Nothing happened.

Frantically Billy jabbed at the button again and again. "I don't understand—why doesn't it work?"

Pirhantis Head tooted on its flute again. The Zords whipped around. They aimed their deadly weapons at the Power Rangers.

"Power Rangers," the wicked fish boomed, "prepare to meet your end!"

CHAPTER 7

"We've got to get out of here!"
Zack shouted.

"No!" Billy cried. "Let me fix the
signal blocker!"

But the Zords were thundering
closer...and closer.

"Hurry, Billy! Hurry!" Kimberly
cried as the Zords' giant shadows
loomed over the Power Rangers.

"I don't believe it!" Billy exclaimed. "I put the batteries in backwards!" He quickly reversed them and pushed the on button.

BUZZZZ! The advancing Zords stopped—seconds before crushing the Power Rangers.

"We got back control of our Zords!" Trini shouted.

"No-o-o!" Lord Zedd howled in rage as he watched from the moon. He raised his staff, and a red light shot toward Earth. It pierced the ground beneath the Power Rangers' feet. The Earth cracked open, and fire rose from the boiling depths of the planet.

The Power Rangers rolled free of the huge crack but watched in horror as six mighty Zords sank slowly into the flaming pit.

"Our Zords!" Jason ran toward the edge of the giant hole. "Tommy, quick! Dragonzord can still break free!"

"I'll send him back to the sea," cried Tommy. He played the secret tune on his flute. Dragonzord struggled and roared, then disappeared into the water's depths.

A grim silence fell over the Power Rangers. Without their old Zords, Zordon couldn't create the new Thunderzords. Without the Thunderzords, they could not defeat Pirhantis Head.

It looked like the end of the Power Rangers—forever!

CHAPTER 8

"**Don't give up yet!**" Zordon called over the Power Rangers' communicators. "Alpha found a way to finish your new Zords."

"Call on them when you're ready," Alpha chimed in.

"Go to it!" Tommy urged.

The Power Rangers stepped forward. "I call upon the power of the Mastodon! Lion Thunder-zord!" Zack shouted.

"I call upon the power of the Triceratops! Unicorn Thunder-zord!" Billy shouted.

"I call upon the power of the Saber-toothed Tiger! Griffin Thunderzord!" Trini shouted.

"I call upon the power of the Pterodactyl! Firebird Thunder-zord!" Kimberly shouted.

"I call upon the power of the Tyrannosaurus! Red Dragon Thunderzord!" Jason shouted.

Instantly the new Zords roared to life. They flew across the stormy sky and raced over the land to help the Power Rangers.

Again the Power Rangers heard

the voice of Zordon. "Now combine the Thunderzords to form one gigantic Mega Thunderzord!"

CLASH! BANG! SLAM! Heavy metal crashed against metal as the Thunderzords united. Bolts snapped into place, and shields locked together. A mighty head rose from its chest. Mega Thunderzord was ready to battle!

The five Power Rangers leaped to their places in the Mega Thunderzord's cockpit. It drew its huge Power Sword and lunged toward Pirhantis Head. Lightning flew from the sword. And Lord Zedd's monster cowered in fear!

From his headquarters on the

moon, Lord Zedd roared, "Grow, Pirhantis Head! Grow!" Lord Zedd stretched out his hand. A small round bomb appeared. With a laugh he hurled it to Earth.

The bomb exploded at his monster's feet. Pirhantis Head began to grow and grow. Taller and taller. Till it stood eye-to-eye with the Mega Thunderzord!

"So you wanna play rough?" the monster shouted. It lifted its fishy flute to its mouth and blew. A stream of fire spewed out. Mega Thunderzord rocked back and forth, but did not fall.

Mega Thunderzord lumbered forward. It held the Power Sword high over Pirhantis Head. Then the sword sliced through the air and came down hard on the ugly monster. The giant fish crashed to the ground. Defeated at last, it sizzled, smoked, and disappeared!

Lord Zedd shook with fury. "Those Power Rangers may have won this time. But I vow I will never rest until their world is completely destroyed!"

The Power Rangers returned to Zordon at the Command Center.

"Congratulations on saving the world," Zordon said proudly. "And on your new beginning."

"These new Zords will serve you well," Alpha said.

"But what's going to happen to

Tommy?" Kimberly asked.

"We don't know yet," Zordon said. "His Dragonzord will need to rest and restore its energy. Just as Tommy's powers will fail him from time to time, so will the Dragonzord's."

"Hey, no sweat," Tommy said. "Being a Power Ranger was nice while it lasted."

"What are you talking about?" Jason said, shaking his head. "You're *always* gonna be one of us."

"Right on," added Billy with a smile.

Tommy grinned. "Thanks, guys."

Suddenly Alpha started to giggle right out loud.

"What's so funny?" Trini asked.

The robot pointed to the viewing globe. Bulk and Skull were zooming backward on the four-wheelers—still trapped under Pirhantis Head's evil spell!

"Whoa-a-a!" Bulk hollered.

The Power Rangers couldn't help but laugh. If only all their problems could be that simple!

The six teens transported to the mountain trail.

Billy pushed the button on his signal blocker, and Bulk and Skull's four-wheelers skidded to a stop.

Tommy and Kimberly dashed

over to see if they were okay.

"Kimberly!" Skull gasped. "Didn't those gray goons get you?"

Tommy and Kimberly pretended to be confused, even though they knew Skull was talking about the Super Putties. "Gray goons? What are you talking about?"

"It was terrible," Skull said. "They surrounded us! But the Power Rangers saved us!"

"No kidding?" said Tommy. "The Power Rangers?"

"We were as close to them as we are to you!" Skull said.

"Oh, really," Kimberly replied. Then she and Tommy shared a secret smile.

The others rode over on their four-wheelers. Bulk and Skull's bikes were useless, so Tommy rode with Kimberly. Skull squeezed in behind Bulk.

"Hey, have you seen a big fish around here?" Skull asked.

"Fish?" Trini asked. "Out here?"

The six friends laughed as they raced back to the trail.

In the distance they heard the cheers for those who had already crossed the finish line. The Power Rangers hadn't come in first, but they were going to finish proudly. They had saved the Earth once again!